Caroline

Glitter Girls

Screen Stars

■SCHOLASTIC

Scholastic Children's Books,
Commonwealth House, 1-19 New Oxford Street,
London WC1A 1NU, UK
a division of Scholastic Ltd

London ~ New York ~ Toronto ~ Sydney ~ Auckland
Mexico City ~ New Delhi ~ Hong Kong

Published by Scholastic Ltd, 2002

Copyright © Caroline Plaisted, 2002

ISBN 0 439 99439 X

Typeset by Falcon Oast Graphic Art Ltd
Printed and bound in Denmark by Nørhaven Paperback A/S, Viborg

4 6 8 10 9 7 5 3

All rights reserved

The right of Caroline Plaisted to be identified as the author
of this work has been asserted by her in accordance
with the Copyright, Designs and Patents Act, 1988.

This book is sold subject to the condition that it shall not,
by way of trade or otherwise, be lent, resold, hired out, or
otherwise circulated without the publisher's prior consent
in any form of binding or cover other than that in which it
is published and without a similar condition, including this
condition, being imposed upon the subsequent purchaser.

Screen Stars

Follow the Glitter Girls' latest adventures!
Collect the other fantastic books in the series:

Chapter 1

It was Friday night and the Glitter Girls were having a sleepover at Meg's house. Charly, Hannah, Zoe, Flo and Meg were busy getting everything ready.

"Right," said Meg, checking off things on her list. "We've got the TV. . ."

"Yes!" said Charly, waving the remote control for the television that the Glitter Girls had borrowed from Meg's sister Sue.

". . .the midnight feast. . ."

"It's here!" smiled Flo, patting a picnic basket that had been filled with all sorts of delicious goodies by her dad.

". . .the drinks. . ."

"Got them!" Hannah held up the cups and

pointed to the bottles of Coke and juice that were sitting on Meg's desk.

". . .is there anything else we need?" Meg asked.

"Don't think so," said Zoe, looking at her watch. "We just need to be ready for the start of ChariTV! The programme starts in about ten minutes!"

"Oh, I can't wait to see Ant and Dec!" said Charly.

Charly dreamed of being a television presenter one day and she especially loved watching anything that starred Ant and Dec. They were her heroes!

"I've got to go to the loo!" said Flo. "Don't start the programme without me!"

Zoe laughed. "Well, hurry up then! We can't ask an entire television channel to wait for you, can we?"

"OK!" Flo giggled, and ran out of the room. The other Glitter Girls settled themselves down on the floor cushions and the bed.

The floor of Meg's bedroom was awash with pillows, sleeping bags, magazines and bags. Each of the Glitter Girls had brought her own bits and pieces to share with the others. Flo had brought some body paints and glitter gels so that she could practise body art on her friends.

Zoe had brought along her scrapbook of pictures of the donkeys at the Donkey Sanctuary. She wanted to show it to the other Glitter Girls because it had some new pictures of Pink and Fluffy, the Glitter Girls' two favourite donkeys.

Hannah had brought a whole load of hair ribbons and braids so she could weave them into the other girls' hair. And Charly had brought along a selection of nail polishes and decorations so that they could all paint their nails!

Just as Flo came back into Meg's bedroom, Charly switched on the television.

"Have I missed anything?" asked Flo, as she leaped across one of the sleeping bags and headed for a free cushion. As she sat down, she popped her thumb into her mouth, as she always did when she was concentrating on something or tired.

"No! It's just starting!" said Charly, pushing her pink glasses back up her nose.

"This is going to be brilliant!" said Zoe, excitedly punching the air as the ChariTV opening music began. . .

★ ♥ ★ ♥ ★ ♥ ★

The Glitter Girls were riveted and watched the programme in silence. It was all about the annual marathon TV programme in aid of Children of the World. Each year it raised vital funds to help poor and needy children all over the globe. First of all, Ant and Dec explained exactly what last year's fund-raising had been spent on. They told everyone about the new schools that had been built in Africa and India and children whose homes had been rebuilt after an earthquake. Then they explained how children in the UK had been helped by various projects. There were new school buses, a special music room for children with sight problems, holidays for children who had never been on holiday before – loads of exciting and really worthwhile projects. It made the Glitter Girls realize how lucky they were.

At the end of the programme, Ant and Dec announced the details of this year's ChariTV telethon. It was going to be held in four weeks' time and they urged everyone watching to do their best to raise money for Children of the World.

"And maybe some of you might even be here with us in the studio in four weeks' time!" said Ant, smiling.

"Yes, the ones who raise the most and the ones who do the most unusual things," Dec explained.

"You can find out more about how to raise money in this week's TV magazines or on the Internet! See you soon!" finished Ant.

"Wow," said Zoe, looking round at the others. "Isn't it amazing how far some of the money goes in the really poor countries?"

"Yes," agreed Meg. "They've managed to help so many children – made their lives so much better, haven't they?"

"I wish we'd been able to help!" said Charly.

"Yes. . ." Hannah said thoughtfully.

Chapter 2

"Come on," Meg said. "I reckon it's time for our feast!"

Without hesitation, the Glitter Girls tucked into the picnic hamper and were soon busy munching and crunching their way through all kinds of delicious food.

"Tell you what," said Hannah, as she chewed on some pizza. "Why don't we do something for ChariTV ourselves this year?"

"Hey – that's a great idea!" Zoe said enthusiastically. "It would be fun!"

"And we need something else to do!" agreed Charly.

The Glitter Girls always liked to have a project on the go. It was one of the things that made being a Glitter Girl so much fun!

"It's true that we need something new for us to do," said Meg slowly and thoughtfully, as she munched on some crisps.

"But we've only recently raised money for Pink and Fluffy, haven't we? It might be difficult to get our parents and friends to support us again so soon," sighed Flo.

"Yes – but we can't let something like ChariTV go by without doing something to help, can we?" Charly pleaded with her friends.

"But what can we do?" asked Zoe. "I mean, we've done sponsored stuff. And we've made things. And held a disco!"

"Yes," Meg joined in. "What else can we do?"

In-between their munching, the Glitter Girls sat thinking about ChariTV. How could they help? They had to think of something different from all the stuff they'd done before. This time they had to come up with something super-cool.

After what seemed like ages, Zoe broke the silence.

"Tell you what," she said. "Why don't we talk to Miss Stanley about it on Monday?"

"Good idea!" agreed Flo. "She's bound to help us think of a way that we can get involved!"

"Yes," agreed Meg. "Why don't we look in the TV magazine for more information about ChariTV tomorrow. We can cut everything out and take it with us to school on Monday to show Miss Stanley."

"Go Glitter!" the others all agreed.

The Glitter Girls bounded into the school play-ground on Monday morning full of fund-raising ideas that they'd had over the weekend.

"I think we should have a mini-marathon!" suggested Meg. "I was talking to my dad about it and he said that a school near where he lives has done something like that recently."

"Sounds fun," said Flo. "But do you think that everyone would want to get involved?"

"That's true," agreed Charly. "I mean, not everyone can run that far."

"And not everyone would want to!" said Hannah.

"Hey!" said Zoe, interrupting the conversation. "There's Miss Stanley going into our classroom now. Let's see if we can catch her before the bell goes!"

And the Glitter Girls raced off to their classroom.

"Hi girls!" said Miss Stanley, smiling at them as she put her bag down on her desk. "You're very keen this morning. What can I do for you?"

"Did you see ChariTV on Friday night, Miss?" Charly asked.

"We cut these out of one of the TV magazines," said Hannah, showing the clippings to her teacher.

Miss Stanley took the bits of paper and sat down. "I did see the programme actually – you were up late, weren't you?"

Miss Stanley looked at the Glitter Girls and then laughed at their worried expressions. "Don't worry! I'm not going to tell you off for staying up late on a Friday! So – why have you brought this in to show me?"

"Well, we wanted help raise some money," Meg explained. "Only we thought that everyone might be a bit fed up with us lot doing more sponsored stuff."

"I mean, we've only just helped the Donkey Sanctuary, haven't we?" Hannah added.

"True," Miss Stanley said thoughtfully. "But it would be good to help raise some money for something as important as this, wouldn't it?"

All the Glitter Girls nodded.

"Can you think of any way that we might be able to help?" Flo asked.

"Well, actually," Miss Stanley said, "we were

talking about ChariTV in the staff room only the other day."

The Glitter Girls looked at each other hopefully and smiled. It had been a good idea to ask Miss Stanley to help them.

Miss Stanley put the magazine clippings down. "We wondered if somehow the whole school could get involved."

"Hey, that's a great idea!" said Charly.

"But what could the whole school do?" Zoe wondered.

"Well, everyone's got lots of talent around here. . ." Miss Stanley said. "Perhaps everyone could offer to do something that they're really good at."

"Good idea!" said Meg. "But how is that going to raise money?"

"I know!" said Flo. "I read about something like this in the paper once! We could hold an Auction of Promises! I think that's what you call it!

"That's a great idea!" said Miss Stanley, beaming at Flo. "Why didn't we think of that before?"

"But what exactly *is* an Auction of Promises?" asked Hannah.

"It's when everyone thinks of something they're really good at – you know, like baking cakes or babysitting, stuff like that – and they offer to do it for nothing. Then someone makes a bid for it, and buys the babysitting or cake. That's how you raise the money," explained Flo.

"What a cool idea!" said Charly.

"Brilliant!" agreed Meg.

"I'll go and ask Mrs Wadhurst about it straight away!" said Miss Stanley.

"Go Glitter!" the girls all said at once. Even Miss Stanley joined in as she walked out of the door.

Chapter 3

Mrs Wadhurst, the Glitter Girls' headteacher, thought it was a fantastic idea too! So the Auction of Promises for ChariTV was on, and the Glitter Girls didn't want to waste a second in helping to get it organized.

"Mrs Wadhurst is going to tell everyone about it at assembly this afternoon," Miss Stanley explained to the girls when she came back from seeing the head. "And she's set a date for the Auction – a week on Friday. That way we can collect all the money that the Promises raise and get it sent in to ChariTV on the night!"

"Yes!" exclaimed Charly and Flo.

"We need to have a meeting to work out what

we're going to do," Meg said, always the first to get organized.

"Well, I'm afraid that'll have to wait until later. It's time for lessons now!" said Miss Stanley, looking at her watch and the queue of children standing outside the classroom.

The Glitter Girls giggled.

"How about after school at my house?" Charly suggested.

"Go Glitter!" came the agreement from her friends.

★ ♥ ★ ♥ ★ ♥ ★

After assembly, the whole school was bubbling with excitement. Almost everyone seemed to have watched ChariTV and there didn't seem to be anyone who wasn't interested in trying to think of a Promise that they could auction.

The teachers had also announced that if everyone brought in a pound then they would dress up as the pop star or TV character of their class's choice on Auction Day! As the children filed out of the hall, discussions were already taking place amongst the children about who their teacher could become on the day of the Auction.

As arranged, the Glitter Girls went back to Charly's house after school. As soon as Mrs Fisher pulled into the drive, the Glitter Girls piled out of the car and raced to the front door.

"I'll have tea ready in about an hour girls. Is that OK?" said Charly's mum as she opened the front door.

"Great! Thanks Mum!" said Charly, as she raced upstairs.

"Thanks Mrs Fisher!" the others called, as they hurried up the stairs behind Charly.

Once they were in Charly's bedroom, the Glitter Girls began their meeting.

"So, what can we promise to do?" Zoe asked.

"We could offer to walk someone's dog!" said Meg.

"Good idea!" agreed Flo.

"But it's not going to make much money, is it?" suggested Hannah.

"True. . ." agreed Charly. "And it's not very exciting."

"We ought to do something we're really good at. . ." said Meg. "Something we can do together. . ."

"And raise loads of money!" added Meg.

"Well, we're good at performing ballets!" said Zoe, remembering the ballet that the Glitter Girls had performed at the local talent competition, and which had won them joint first prize!

"I've got it!" said Hannah.

"What?" asked Charly.

"We could do a makeover for someone!" Hannah suggested. "Like we did at the school fête. Only we could just makeover one person this time!"

"Yeah," said Flo. "But wouldn't it be even

better if we did a whole group of people? You know, a group of girls just like us!" Flo added.

"We could promise a Makeover Party!" said Meg.

"That sounds like a perfect Promise!" agreed Flo.

"Right, now we need to get our families sorted out," said Meg, reaching for her notebook.

"Yes, they need to make Promises too!" Hannah agreed.

"Let's ask them tonight!" said Flo.

"Go Glitter!" they all screamed excitedly.

The Glitter Girls got together in the playground at break the next day to talk about the other Promises.

"My dad says he'll cook a Chinese meal for four!" said Flo.

"And my mum says she'll bake a cake a week

for someone, for the whole term!" Charly stated.

"My mum says that if we help her, she'll do a designer job on someone's room – you know, a complete room makeover with new curtains and cushions and stuff!" said Hannah.

"Fantastic – I'd bid for that!" said Meg. "My brother said he'd give someone a snooker lesson."

"And my sister said she'd paint a T-shirt to someone's design," said Flo, whose big sister Kim was really brilliant at art.

"Help!" said Meg, pulling a pink pad and pencil from her pocket. "I'd better write all these down before we forget them!"

As she started to scribble, the other Glitter Girls listed all of the things that they'd thought of that could be promised at the Auction.

"I spoke to my dad on the phone and he thought he might be able to redesign some-one's garden for them," said Meg.

"I'll have a word with my sisters tonight," said Zoe, "and see if I can get them to do something."

"This is going to be a great Auction, isn't it?" said Flo, and the others all agreed with her.

"I wonder who'll do the actual Auction?" said Charly. "Do you think it'll be one of the teachers? I mean, it's a really important job."

"I've no clue!" said Flo. "But I hope it's someone really cool!"

"Like Ant and Dec!" said Charly.

"Get real," said Zoe, laughing.

Just then the bell went, beckoning everyone back into school.

"I'll put it on my list to talk about at our next meeting," Meg suggested, following the other Glitter Girls back into their classroom.

Chapter 4

The Glitter Girls never met up on Tuesday afternoons because that was when Flo and Charly had their swimming lesson and Meg had her cello lesson. But that didn't stop the Glitter Girls from talking about ChariTV with their families when they all got home that night!

So by the time they arrived at school on Wednesday, they were full of new ideas.

"I thought we could go to the bookshop in town and ask if they've got any signed copies of books that we could auction," Zoe said enthusiastically.

"Sounds cool," Flo replied. "I wondered if the steam railway would let us have some free tickets."

"I wondered about exactly the same thing!" said Hannah. "And I thought that maybe some of the restaurants in town could be persuaded to offer free meals."

"It's worth a try," said Meg, as she scribbled the ideas down.

"Seems to me," said Charly, "that we need to take a trip around town one afternoon after school."

"Excellent!" replied Hannah.

"Yes – let's ask Miss Stanley about it," said Zoe.

★ ♥ ★ ♥ ★ ♥ ★

Miss Stanley was equally enthusiastic about the Glitter Girls' idea to get local shops and businesses to join in with the Auction of Promises.

"That would be such a help, girls! You will let me know how you get on – perhaps you could make me a list? Then I could let Mrs Wadhurst know what's been promised," said Miss Stanley.

"No problem," replied Meg.

"Is someone keeping a record of all the Promises that are being offered?" Zoe asked.

Miss Stanley furrowed her brow. "I'm not sure that they are. And you're right – someone ought to be keeping a record so that we know exactly what we've got for the actual Auction. We need someone to be the main point of contact – the main organizer to keep us all on our toes."

"Well, why don't we do it?" Flo suggested. "It would be easy, wouldn't it?" she said, looking round at her friends.

"Yes – easy peasy," agreed Hannah.

"No problem!" Meg added, an organizing twinkle in her eye. "We could put everything up on the noticeboard in reception so that everyone knows what's going on."

"Excellent, girls!" Miss Stanley smiled at them. "I can always rely on you Glitter Girls to help, can't I?" she looked at the clock on the classroom wall. "Now I think it's time for you all to get on with some work."

"Yes Miss!" they all said at once.

★ ♥ ★ ♥ ★ ♥ ★

At lunchtime, Hannah, Zoe, Flo, Meg and Charly got a chance to talk.

"We've got to make this the best ChariTV ever," said Hannah.

"Certainly have," agreed Charly.

"Who do you think Mrs Wadhurst will ask to do the Auction?" Flo asked.

Mrs Wadhurst had told the girls that morning that the mayoress had offered to do everything she could to help with the Auction. She was going to get all the local councillors to come along and had suggested the Town Hall for the venue so they could get the biggest audience!

"The auctioneer's got to be someone who's really good at talking to the public and making it fun and stuff," said Meg.

"It'd be so cool if they could get someone really well known," Meg said, chewing the end of her pink pencil.

"Like a television star or an actor," said Charly, pushing her pink glasses back up her nose thoughtfully.

"I could speak to my mum," suggested Hannah, "see who's working at the theatre at the moment."

"Brilliant idea!" said Zoe.

"Cool!" agreed the others enthusiastically.

"Go Glitter!" they cried!

★ ♥ ★ ♥ ★ ♥ ★

After tea, Hannah sat in the kitchen with her mum, and explained their idea about getting a celebrity auctioneer.

"So might you know someone who could help?" she asked.

"Well, we've got some rehearsals going on at the moment for a new play that opens next month," said Mrs Giles, sipping her drink. "It would be nice to have someone young, wouldn't it?"

Hannah's mum had a knowing smile on her face. It was an expression that Hannah knew well and it meant that she was on to something!

"Who are you thinking of, Mum?" Hannah grinned at her, desperate to know who it was.

"Well – of course she might not be free to do it – it is less than two weeks away after all. . ." Hannah's mum frowned at the thought.

"Who, Mum?" Hannah pleaded impatiently.

Her mum laughed. "Well, we've got a lovely girl who's acting in the play – someone who everyone would know. . ."

"So who *is* she?!" Hannah squeaked.

"The actress who plays Sonia," Mrs Giles said putting her cup down on the table in front of her, "in *EastEnders*."

"Sonia! She'd be perfect!" screamed Hannah excitedly. "I must go and tell the others!"

Hannah got up from the table and dashed over to the phone.

"Hannah!" Mrs Giles called to her. "Don't get too excited! She may not be able to make it! And I haven't even asked her yet!"

"I know!" said Hannah, grinning with excitement. "But an idea like this can't wait until tomorrow! I've got to phone everyone now!"

Chapter 5

RAT-tat-tat!

Charly was in her bedroom waiting for the other Glitter Girls to arrive. Her face lit up as she heard the familiar knock.

"Who is it?" Charly whispered.

"GG!" came the response.

She opened the door and there stood Hannah, Zoe, Flo and Meg – they'd all arrived at the same time.

"Have you heard from Sonia?" Charly asked Hannah anxiously, as she took off her special Glitter Girl jacket. The others were dressed exactly the same in their jackets and soon there was a pile of them on the chair near Charly's desk.

The Glitter Girls had been ecstatic when Hannah had phoned them the evening before to tell them about her mum's brilliant idea.

"It's too soon to know," explained Hannah, as she sat down on Charly's fluffy bedside rug. "Mum will only have been able to ask her today because she had to check it out with Mrs Wadhurst first. Oh, and by the way, her real name's Natalie Cassidy."

"It would be just great if she says yes!" said Flo, hugging her knees to her chest as she spoke. As she moved, the tiny chain of silver and pink bells that were hanging from her hair-clip chimed.

"Anyway, we brought some munchies up with us!" said Zoe, handing round a plate of veggies and dip.

"And some lemonade!" added Flo. "I'm starving! Hey, cute trousers Charly!"

It was Thursday afternoon and the Glitter Girls were meeting up after school, but they'd all had just enough time to go home and change before they started their meeting.

Charly's trousers were new and she was very proud of them. "Thanks," she said, smiling. The trousers were bright pink and had a mass of beads and sequins decorating them. "Mum did them for me – she found the trousers in the market and then I helped her customize them. They're cool, aren't they?"

"They're gorgeous!" agreed Zoe. "And they go really well with your jacket!"

"Come on – we've got lots to do," said Meg, settling herself down on Charly's Groovy Chick duvet cover and taking her pen and notebook out of her pocket. "So – how did you all get on today?"

Usually, the Glitter Girls stuck together at school and hung around with each other at break and lunchtime. But today had been different. Today, the Glitter Girls had organized a special meeting in the hall after lunch. Each of them had sat at a table whilst everyone at school, even some of the teachers, had queued up to tell them what Promises they were going to auction for ChariTV.

"OK, I'll start. . ." said Hannah, twiddling her hair round her finger as she always did when she was thinking, and the Glitter Girls began to go through the lists they'd each drawn up.

★ ♥ ★ ♥ ★ ♥ ★

Half an hour later, Zoe finished reading out her list – hers was the last one.

"Well," said Meg, looking through her note-book, "there are about a hundred Promises here!"

"Isn't it fantastic?" said Zoe. "I mean, special meals being cooked, cakes, a bedspread, room makeovers, snooker, a tap class, riding and tennis and football lessons. . ."

Hannah carried on the list, ". . .a magical makeover party, a trip in a vintage car, a customized T-shirt. . ."

". . .a valet, a video recording of a special event, someone to care for your pets while you're away on holiday. . ." Flo said.

". . .and then," added Charly, "there will be the money raised by the teachers for dressing up. And there's that girl in Year Six whose dad is going to get sponsored for running a marathon!"

"Hey – don't forget we've still got to go round town and see if we can get some more Promises from the shops and businesses," Zoe said. "That should get a lot more things to Auction!"

"And a lot more money, too!" agreed Flo.

Meg closed her notebook with a satisfied smile. "Maybe we could go into town tomorrow after school. Then we can type up our final list on the computer afterwards."

"Yeah! Then we can give it to Miss Stanley on Monday!" Charly said.

Just then, the Glitter Girls were interrupted

by a faint RAT-tat-tat! at Charly's bedroom door.

"Hey – was that the door?" Charly whispered.

"It sounded like a knock – one of our knocks," said Zoe.

"But it was really faint!" said Flo.

RAT-tat-tat! This time the knock was a little bolder.

Charly got up and made her way over to the door.

"Who is it?" she whispered, puzzled. But there was no reply. Overcome with impatience and curiosity, Charly opened the door, only to find her little sister Lily standing there. Lily had a broad grin on her face.

"GG!" she said, happy to be a Glitter Girl even for just a few minutes. "Time for tea!"

★　♥　★　♥　★　♥　★

On Friday afternoon, the Glitter Girls went home to change and put on their Glitter Girl jackets before going back into town with

Charly's mum. They'd designed a special leaflet on the computer which explained all about the Auction for ChariTV. Charly's mum accompanied the Glitter Girls as they set off on their trail around town.

"Right," said Meg, organizing everyone. "Let's start this end, go up this side of the street and then cross over at the top and come down the other side."

"Go Glitter!" the other four friends replied.

An hour and a half later, the Glitter Girls stood outside the chemist's by the traffic lights, tired but extremely pleased with themselves. They'd visited all the major stores – and had even gone into the library, the museum and the ticket office at the old town Steam Railway Station.

"What a success!" said Hannah.

"Definitely!" agreed Flo.

"We did OK, didn't we?" said Zoe, tucking her plait behind her ear.

Meg looked at the list in her notebook and read it aloud.

"A trip on the steam train, a selection of perfume from the chemist's, a food hamper from the supermarket, a voucher for a coach trip to the zoo from the coach station," Meg paused and pushed a wisp of her long, wavy blonde hair out of her eyes, ". . .free meals in some of the restaurants, a barrel of beer, free haircuts for a whole family and a private swimming party at the leisure centre."

"Result!" said Charly, punching the air with her fist.

"You did brilliantly, girls," agreed Mrs Fisher. "Well done!"

"Now we need to get posters in all the shops so that absolutely everyone knows about the Auction of Promises," said Flo.

"Go Glitter!" said Lily from her pushchair.

And Zoe, Hannah, Charly, Meg and Flo had to agree!

Chapter 6

On Saturday morning, Hannah raced around to Flo's house, where the Glitter Girls had agreed to meet up. Hannah was desperate to see the girls. Her mum had just received a phone call and Hannah couldn't wait to tell her best friends what it was all about!

"Hey, you're in a hurry," said Kim, Flo's sister, who was helping the girls to scan in the ChariTV logo on the computer so that they could use it when they typed up the Promises.

"I certainly am!" agreed Hannah.

"So what's up?" asked Meg, who had already arrived with the others in Flo's bedroom.

"She's said yes! Sonia – I mean, Natalie! She's agreed to do it!" Hannah was beaming with happiness. Now the ChariTV auction was complete!

"Wow! that's fantastic!" said Meg.

"Totally brilliant!" screamed Zoe.

"Sonia! Yesss!" said Flo.

"So cool!" Charly jumped up and down.

"Now we can do the posters as well!" said Meg. "We can get on with everything today."

"Go Glitter!" they all screamed at once.

The Glitter Girls spent a busy morning working on their list. Flo used hearts and stars to decorate the border around the list. And she positioned the ChariTV logo at the top of the page.

"Doesn't it look good?" said Meg, holding up the bits of paper to admire it with her friends. The list was so long that it went over three pages.

"Fantastic," agreed Hannah.

"Thanks Flo!" said Zoe.

"Now we've got to do the posters as well!" said Flo.

Flo and her sister designed a basic poster using the ChariTV logo and the list of Promises. All the Glitter Girls then coloured and decorated each poster individually. They used an assortment of fluorescent gel inks and glittery pens that Kim and Flo had in their art box.

By the end of the morning, the Glitter Girls had decorated twenty-five posters, and sat back to admire their handiwork.

"Do you think we've done enough?" Charly asked.

"There's a lot of shops in town," Hannah said, pulling her long silky red hair out of its ponytail which had been keeping it out of the way while she worked.

"She's right," Meg agreed, her own blonde curls tied back with a scrunchie covered in pink and purple feathers.

"I know!" said Flo. "Let's take a couple into the Print Shop and see if they'll photocopy some more for us! They can do colour – I remember Kim got something done for a project."

"Great idea!" said Meg. "Let's do it when we take the posters into town."

"Go Glitter!" her friends replied.

★ ♥ ★ ♥ ★ ♥ ★

Meg's dad took the Glitter Girls into town that afternoon. The Print Shop did kindly agree to copy more posters – in fact they doubled the amount of posters and didn't charge the girls anything, seeing as it was for such a good cause! By the time the Glitter Girls had been down the high street, almost every shop had put up a poster in their window and lots of the shopkeepers had promised to come to the Auction too!

On Monday, the Glitter Girls put up posters at

school and Mrs Wadhurst held one up at assembly.

"The poster says 'Special Celebrity Auctioneer – Natalie Cassidy, also known as Sonia from *EastEnders*'," said Mrs Wadhurst. "Let's make sure that we have the best ChariTV event in the country! It's on Friday evening, boys and girls – at the Town Hall!" Mrs Wadhurst reminded everyone.

Everyone had cheered and agreed that they'd tell everyone they knew to come to the Auction. The Glitter Girls were beside themselves with anticipation. They'd never known everyone in the school to be quite so excited about an event before. The atmosphere was brilliant.

★ ♥ ★ ♥ ★ ♥ ★

On the day of the Auction, the teachers turned up dressed as the characters that their classes had chosen for them! They looked great. Some came as TV characters – Mrs Wadhurst came as

Dot Cotton, which the girls thought was hilarious. Others came as footballers, witches or pop stars. The Glitter Girls' class had decided that Miss Stanley should come dressed as Marge Simpson and she had really gone to town on her costume! She even had an enormous wig piled on top of her head and great big earrings!

★ ♥ ★ ♥ ★ ♥ ★

After school, the Glitter Girls raced to Charly's house to have tea quickly and then get ready. It had been decided that the people who were making the Promises should stand up as the Promises were being bid for. So the Glitter Girls had chosen to look their best as an advert for the Magical Makeover Party that they were offering.

Of course, all of them were wearing their Glitter Girl jackets, but Meg was wearing a purple mini-skirt with a pink halterneck top.

Hannah had decided to wear her favourite denim pedal pushers which had silvery flowers sewn all over them that matched her T-shirt.

Charly was wearing the bootleg trousers that her mum had recently customized for her and Zoe had chosen a really cool pair of jeans and a stripy boob tube. Flo was wearing a white crop top with a cute short flared skirt – it had three layers of frill and each one was a different colour of pink.

The Glitter Girls had a great time helping each other with their hair and painting each others' nails with glitter polish.

"Are you girls ready?" Charly's mum called up the stairs. She'd arranged to take them to the Auction and wait for the rest of their families there.

"It's six o'clock!" said Meg, looking at her watch.

"Go Glitter!" the girls all called, and zoomed downstairs to get on their way.

★ ♥ ★ ♥ ★ ♥ ★

By six thirty, the Town Hall was buzzing with people. The Auction was due to start at seven o'clock and Hannah's mum had arranged to bring Natalie with her, straight from rehearsals at the theatre. Hannah, Flo, Zoe, Charly and Meg couldn't wait to meet her – they loved her character in *EastEnders*!

"Hey, look!" said Charly, as they walked in. "There's Miss Stanley!"

The Glitter Girls waved to their teacher, still in her fancy dress like all of the other teachers, from across the hall. When Miss Stanley saw the Glitter Girls, she waved enthusiastically, looking just as excited as them.

"Isn't this exciting?" Miss Stanley said as she came over.

"It's going to be the best evening ever!" said Zoe.

"Do you know girls, I think you're right!"

agreed Miss Stanley. "Look how many people are here already!"

"We'd better get some seats," said Meg. "Before it's too late!"

"Have a good evening girls!" Miss Stanley said as they went off.

Flo found them a whole row of seats fairly near to the front and the girls sat down, saving extra seats for their families.

"Phew! It's almost done," said Meg, having a quick look at her notepad.

"Have we forgotten anything?" said Hannah, looking over Meg's shoulder.

After a few seconds, Meg flipped the pad shut. "No – I think we've done our bit!" she said. "Mr Wix is sitting at the front to write down who buys what and how much they're paying. Now we've just got to wait for Sonia to arrive!"

Chapter 7

With only ten minutes to go, the Town Hall was packed with people! In fact, there were so many that some people were having to stand at the back.

"I wonder where Mum is," said Hannah, looking at her watch. "It's not like her to leave it so late."

"She's probably with Sonia, I mean Natalie, outside now!" said Charly, wondering if she would get the chance to speak to the actress later.

By now, the Glitter Girls had been joined by the rest of their families and with the hall so full, the empty seat that they had saved for Mrs Giles was very obvious.

Suddenly, Dr Baker's mobile phone rang.

"Ooops! I hope that's not the hospital. . ." said Dr Baker, standing up and moving over to the side of the hall to answer.

A few minutes later, she was back, with a worried expression on her face.

"What's up, Mum?" Zoe asked.

"That was your mum, Hannah," Dr Baker said. "I'm afraid Natalie's got a throat infection and her doctor has told her that she shouldn't do the Auction tonight. I'm so sorry girls. . ."

The Glitter Girls were distraught. If Sonia wasn't going to do the Auction of Promises then who *was* going to run it? They couldn't cancel everything now! They had to raise the money for ChariTV!

★ ♥ ★ ♥ ★ ♥ ★

"What can we do?" Charly asked. "I mean, who else can do the Auction?"

Meg looked at her four friends, a smile slowly

appearing on her face.

"Who are you thinking of?" asked Hannah, recognizing Meg's expression as the one she had when she'd thought of a really brilliant idea.

"Yes – tell us!" pleaded Flo.

Meg was now beaming. "Us!" she said simply. "We could do it! The Glitter Girls could do the Auction!"

The remaining four Glitter Girls looked at each other for a second and then they too broke into smiles!

"Let's go and speak to Mrs Wadhurst now!" said Flo, buzzing with excitement.

"Go Glitter!" they all said at once.

★ ♥ ★ ♥ ★ ♥ ★

"It's a terrible shame about Natalie," said Mrs Wadhurst, when she heard the news. "But do you think you can manage to run the Auction?" Mrs Wadhurst asked them.

"Course we can!" said Charly.

Mrs Wadhurst laughed but still looked uncertain.

"Oh pleeeease, Mrs Wadhurst!" said Hannah.

"We'd love to help out!" agreed Zoe.

"Yes, pleeeeeeease!" said Meg.

Mrs Wadhurst looked at the Glitter Girls' eager faces.

"OK, girls," she smiled at them. "Here's the list that you made for Natalie, to help her with the Auction. We've added the amount that we hope to get for each Promise. Right, let's get going. I'll explain to everyone what's happened and then introduce the Glitter Girls!"

"Go Glitter!" the five friends exclaimed.

★ ♥ ★ ♥ ★ ♥ ★

A few minutes later, Mrs Wadhurst walked on to the stage. With so many people there, the chattering and laughter was deafening. Gradually, the room fell silent.

"Well – welcome to our ChariTV Auction of Promises," Mrs Wadhurst began.

Everyone in the audience cheered like mad!

"Now, I've got some bad news, I'm afraid. Poor Natalie Cassidy, the actress who plays Sonia Jackson in *EastEnders*, can't be with us tonight. . ." There were disappointed murmurs throughout the Town Hall as Mrs Wadhurst explained the situation. "But there's good news as well!" Mrs Wadhust continued. "I think most of you know the Glitter Girls and how much they've done to help organize this evening."

There was cheering of approval from the audience.

"Well – the Glitter Girls have offered to do the Auction instead!"

Everyone cheered and clapped as the Glitter Girls made their way to join Mrs Wadhurst on the stage. Now they could see everyone – even the people at the back. And everyone could see them!

Hannah squeezed Charly's hand with excitement. "I think you should go first!" she whispered to her friend. "You'll be the best at this!"

"Is that OK with everyone else?" Charly asked, desperate to get going.

"Go Glitter!" they all whispered back.

Mrs Wadhurst turned to the Glitter Girls. "Ready?" she asked, smiling.

They nodded.

A microphone had been placed at the front and Charly walked up to it confidently, beamed a smile at the audience and said, "Good evening everyone! My name's Charly and I am one of the Glitter Girls! And these are my friends, Hannah, Meg, Flo and Zoe. Welcome to the first Wells Road School ChariTV Auction of Promises. We've got lots of fantastic Promises for you to bid for tonight. So please spend lots and lots of money to support ChariTV!"

The audience erupted into applause again.

"Right," said Charly. "The first Promise we are auctioning tonight is a Chinese supper for four. Courtesy of top local Chinese food expert, Flo's dad – er, I mean, Mr Eng!"

The audience laughed and cheered. Mr Eng, who had until now been busy recording the Glitter Girls' big moment with his videocam, stood up and waved his hands in the air.

"Who will give me fifty pounds?" Charly asked.

The ChariTV Auction of Promises had begun!

Chapter 8

The next couple of hours passed in a frenzy of excitement and fun. Charly managed to auction the Chinese meal for over a hundred pounds and after that the five Glitter Girls took it in turns to auction all of the Promises. Hannah sold her mum's offer of a Changing Rooms Special for nearly two hundred pounds! All of the other items sold for well over the price that Mrs Wadhurst and the teachers had anticipated. The Glitter Girls were having the most fantastic time – and, judging by the cheers and laughter from the audience, so was *everyone* in the Town Hall!

Finally, there was only one item left to auction. It was the Glitter Girls' own Promise of the Magical Makeover Party!

"Who wants to bid for our Magical Makeover Party?" Charly asked the audience.

"We're offering a makeover for up to six girls," explained Hannah.

"We'll do hair braiding, nail art and body art!" added Flo.

"So who'll start the bidding at twenty pounds?" Zoe asked, looking around the room hopefully.

To their surprise, Miss Stanley put up her hand!

"I'll give you thirty!" she said.

"Fifty!" said Mrs Wadhurst. The Glitter Girls couldn't believe it! Their own teachers were bidding for the Magical Makeover Party!

"Sixty pounds!" said Mrs Bugden, the school cook.

The audience was loving it! The Glitter Girls could hardly get a word in. It seemed like every teacher in the school was making a bid for the

Glitter Girls' Promise. Even Mr Render, the Deputy Head!

"A hundred pounds!" said Mrs Wadhurst, standing up to applause from the cheering audience. "That's my final offer!"

The Glitter Girls looked at each other, laughing with delight at their success.

Charly took hold of the microphone and grinned at the audience. "Ladies and gentlemen! We have an offer for a hundred pounds! Going once?"

She looked around at the sea of smiles.

"Going twice? At a hundred pounds!"

Charly checked again, just in case anyone dared to outbid Mrs Wadhurst.

"Going three times?"

No one stirred. The Glitter Girls all looked at each other with delight.

"The Glitter Girls' Magical Makeover Party is sold to Mrs Wadhurst for one hundred pounds! Go Glitter!"

"Go Glitter!" everyone in the audience shouted back!

★ ♥ ★ ♥ ★ ♥ ★

As everyone chattered away in their seats, Mrs Wadhurst made her way up on to the stage again.

"Well, everyone! What an amazing evening this has been! And what would we have done without the Glitter Girls?" she said. "Let's give them a big round of applause!"

Everyone clapped and cheered and the Glitter Girls hugged each other with happiness.

Mrs Wadhurst waited for everyone to quieten down before carrying on.

"Well, Mr Wix has been keeping a tally of just how much money we have raised for ChariTV this evening. . ." she said, looking down at the piece of paper she was clutching in her hand, ". . .and I am thrilled to tell you that we have raised just over four thousand pounds between us!"

The whole place exploded with cheering . . . and the Glitter Girls stared at each other in amazement.

"So," said Mrs Wadhurst, "while we hope that Natalie Cassidy feels better soon –" the audience clapped in agreement "– we've all had a wonderful evening here tonight. And I'm sure that we are going to have the most wonderful time taking up our Promises over the next week or so . . . let's wish ChariTV every success!"

★ ♥ ★ ♥ ★ ♥ ★

Mrs Wadhurst was right when she said that everyone was going to have fun with the Promises. Flo's dad, Mr Eng, had made a video of the actual Auction and he then spent as much time as he could over the next week videoing people carrying out their Promises.

The very next day after the Auction, some of the boys at school held their five-a-side football party and Mr Eng stood on the sidelines filming it.

Then, on the Saturday afternoon, the Glitter Girls went with Mr Eng to film their classmate's dad finishing his marathon!

The Glitter Girls went with Mr Eng as often as they could over the next week. And every time, the Glitter Girls went home knowing that everything about the Auction of Promises had been worth it.

Chapter 9

There were two weeks to go before the big ChariTV night on the television, and at the end of the first week it was time for the Glitter Girls to makeover their teachers!

When the Glitter Girls arrived in the staff room after school on Friday, Hannah, Flo, Meg, Charlie and Zoe were met by Miss Stanley, Mrs Wadhurst, Mrs Bugden, and two other teachers from Reception and Year One, Mrs Bates and Miss Crane.

"We've been looking forward to this all week," smiled Miss Stanley. "Now, who's going to do my nails? I want to make sure I look really fantastic for the party I'm going to tomorrow!"

"Me!" said Zoe, bouncing over to Miss

Stanley. "Now, these are all the colours," Zoe got a shoebox absolutely full of all different shades of nail polish out of her bag and laid it down on the table. "And these are the decorations we can put on top."

There were all sorts of shimmering stars and tiny jewels to choose from.

"Oh – don't they just look gorgeous!" Miss Stanley said.

After a few minutes, she picked out a blueypurple colour to be decorated with silver moons.

In the meantime, Mrs Wadhurst was having a tattoo put on her arm by Meg. She'd chosen a really pretty flower design.

Hannah was busy braiding some red ribbon into Miss Crane's long, dark-brown hair and Flo was also busy doing Mrs Bugden's nails.

"I'll have to make sure I wear my rubber gloves in the school kitchen on Monday, won't I?" she laughed. "I don't want to spoil all your hard work and my pretty fingers!"

Charly was on the other side of the room with Mrs Bates, who was having a little spray of silvery bells tied carefully at the side of her blonde fringe.

By the end of the afternoon, the Glitter Girls had each taken it in turns to makeover all of the teachers and Mr Eng, who had been at the makeover at the very beginning, had come back to film the end result.

"So have you enjoyed it?" Mr Eng asked the teachers from behind the camcorder.

"Go Glitter!" the teachers all called at once, their arms raised in true Glitter Girl style above their heads.

"Go Glitter!" the Glitter Girls replied enthusiastically!

On Saturday night, Mr Eng filmed his own stint at cooking a special Chinese meal for a family.

It turned out to be Meg's mum who was the successful bidder for that Promise! And, as an extra-special treat, she asked Mr Eng if he would cook for all the Glitter Girls as well as Meg's family. So he did! It was such a brilliant evening and at the end of it, from behind his camcorder, Mr Eng asked everyone to cheer to the camera. "GOOD LUCK CHARITV!" they all cried in unison.

On Monday, the Glitter Girls took the finished video recording into school. With the help of Miss Stanley, it was packaged up and sent with a letter and the cheque for the money raised to ChariTV at their studios. The whole school had sent a letter explaining everything that had been done.

"Do you think we'll hear from Ant and Dec?" Charly asked her friends.

"I expect we'll get a thank you letter after the programme, don't you?" Meg replied.

"I should think so," agreed Flo.

"I hope so," said Zoe.

After the excitement of the last few weeks, everything suddenly seemed a bit flat. . .

★ ♥ ★ ♥ ★ ♥ ★

At last, it was Friday morning. Only one day to go until ChariTV was on TV! Everyone at school was still talking about all of the Promises that had happened – even the teachers!

At breaktime, Miss Stanley came rushing over to Hannah, Zoe, Meg, Flo and Charly in the playground.

"I've just come straight from Mrs Wadhurst's office . . . she's had a phone call . . . from the TV studio . . . about our Auction!" said Miss Stanley, a little out of breath.

"Have they received our cheque then?" asked Zoe.

Miss Stanley beamed at the girls. "They certainly have," she said, "and our video! In fact, the video is one of the reasons they called! They want to use it in the programme on Saturday night!"

"Wow!" said Zoe and Flo at the same time.

"Brilliant!" screamed Hannah.

"Yess!" said Meg.

"That's so cool!" said Charly.

"But there's more to it!" said Miss Stanley. "They want us to go along to the TV studios to present the cheque!"

"What cheque?" asked Meg. "We already sent it, didn't we?"

"Well, yes we did," Miss Stanley replied, "But apparently they are having a giant version of the cheque made so that it can be held up in the television studio."

"Oh, I've seen those on TV before," said Flo.

"But who's going to the TV studio?" Meg repeated.

"Us!" Miss Stanley replied. "I mean – me, Mrs Wadhurst . . . and you, girls!"

"What?" Charly asked, hardly daring to believe what she'd just heard.

"Us?" the other Glitter Girls said together, in astonishment.

"Well, they liked Mr Eng's video and the ideas behind the Auction of Promises so much," Miss Stanley explained, "that they've asked someone to go along from the school. And Mrs Wadhurst thinks that, as you were the ones who had the idea for the Auction, and helped to organize it, it ought to be you!"

"Go Glitter!" the Glitter Girls screamed with delight. They could hardly believe it – they were going to be on telly!

Chapter 10

On Saturday afternoon, the Glitter Girls found themselves on a train to London with Miss Stanley and Mrs Wadhurst. They were on their way to take part in ChariTV, which was going to be broadcast live that very night!

The girls were all wearing their special Glitter Girl T-shirts and jackets, which looked really eye-catching. Zoe had the cuffs of her Glitter Girl jacket folded back to reveal the shimmery body lotion she'd applied. And they were all wearing the same silver and pink trainers – they'd seen them in Girl's Dream and hadn't been able to resist!

But the Glitter Girls were all carrying extra T-shirts with them – and felt pens. They'd been given them by Hannah's mum. They weren't ordinary felt pens though – they were special ones that could write on fabric, and Hannah's mum had suggested that they got all the stars they met at ChariTV to sign their T-shirts! Then they would have a special memento of their evening! The Glitter Girls thought it was such a cool idea and couldn't wait to meet the stars.

"Only fifteen minutes till we're there!" said Mrs Wadhurst.

As soon as they arrived at Waterloo station, they hopped into a taxi for the short journey to the TV studios.

"Off to make a programme, are you?" the taxi driver asked, smiling at the Glitter Girls.

"Yes," explained Charly. "We're going to be on ChariTV tonight!"

"ChariTV, eh?" he said. "I'll have to look out for you when I watch then! Here we are. . ."

The taxi pulled up outside an enormous building and the Glitter Girls piled out.

"Have a good time then, girls!" he called. "What's it say on the back of your jackets?" he asked.

"GG," said Meg. "It stands for Glitter Girls!"

"So I've had the Glitter Girls in my taxi, then?" he laughed. "I'll remember you when you're famous!"

"Go Glitter!" the girls replied!

★ ♥ ★ ♥ ★ ♥ ★

A really nice girl called Trudy met them in reception. She explained that she was the Production Assistant on the programme. She took the Glitter Girls and their teachers over to join another larger group of people. They were all people who had helped raise money for ChariTV, just like the Glitter Girls.

"Right," said Trudy. "We're going to show everyone around the studio itself first and then you'll all go down to the canteen for something to eat before the programme broadcasts. When it's your turn to present your cheque, I'll cue you on to the set and you can have a quick chat with Ant and Dec."

"You mean we actually get to meet Ant and Dec?" Zoe asked in wonderment.

"Certainly do!" said Trudy.

"Go Glitter!" the girls exclaimed.

Trudy laughed at their excitement. "We'll have to get you to do that on film! Now – wait here with everyone else and Poppy will come down in a minute to show you round. See you later – bye!"

"Bye!" the Glitter Girls replied.

A tour round the studio? A live TV show? Meeting Ant and Dec? What a Glitter Girl adventure this was turning out to be!

Poppy showed them around the studio and

explained about the cameras and the make-up girls. Everyone was going to be made-up so that they would look perfect on the show! There were five other girls in their group, about the same age as the Glitter Girls. When they went down to the canteen, the Glitter Girls ended up sitting next to them.

"So, how did you get to be here?" one of the girls asked. She had a Scottish accent, like the other girls in her gang, and short blonde hair.

Flo explained about the Auction of Promises. "How about you?" she asked.

"We did a sponsored swim. We swam all day and all night in a relay. We got to come down because we were the youngest in the swimming squad," explained one of them.

"All day and all night?" marvelled Zoe. "You must be really good swimmers!"

"Oh – we did OK," another of the girls smiled.

Just then, Meg interrupted. "Hey!" she said. "Isn't that Sonia from *EastEnders* over there?"

The other Glitter Girls looked round to where Meg was pointing. She was right!

"Come on!" said Charly. "Let's go over and speak to her!"

"Can we, Miss Stanley?" Zoe asked their teacher.

Miss Stanley smiled at the girls. "Of course you can – only don't disturb her for too long!"

"See you in a minute!" Hannah said to their new friends.

And the Glitter Girls rushed off.

★ ♥ ★ ♥ ★ ♥ ★

"I was so sorry I couldn't make it to your school," Natalie said. "It sounds like you had a great night!"

The Glitter Girls had explained who they were and where they had come from.

"We're really looking forward to seeing you in the play!" Meg said.

"Yes – Hannah's mum's got tickets for us!" explained Zoe.

"Well, you'll have to come backstage and see me when you come!" said Natalie, smiling. "So, are you having a good time today?"

The Glitter Girls all nodded their heads.

"We're really looking forward to meeting Ant and Dec," said Charly.

"You'll meet lots of other people as well tonight," said Natalie.

"Would you sign our T-shirts?" Hannah asked, offering one of the special pens to Natalie. Then she explained the story behind the T-shirts.

"What a great idea!" said Natalie, and then one by one, she signed all the girls' T-shirts. "Mrs Giles told me that one of you wants to be a television presenter. Which one of you is it?"

"Me!" beamed Charly, flicking her hair behind her shoulders.

"Well, don't be too good tonight," Natalie laughed. "Or you'll do Ant and Dec out of a job!"

Chapter 11

Not long after, Trudy came back to find the Glitter Girls and their new Scottish friends chatting away.

"We've got to go down to make-up," she explained, leading them out of the canteen and along a corridor.

All of them were fascinated by their journey. They passed so many interesting people – actors they recognized from soaps, newsreaders, sports presenters – all sorts! And there were intriguing signs on the doors like "Studio 8" and "Production Wardrobe".

At last they arrived at a door marked "Make-Up 4" and Trudy whisked them inside.

"These young ladies and their teachers are

here for ChariTV," Trudy explained to the three girls who were in the room. "I'll be back for you all in twenty minutes!"

Trudy zoomed off and the make-up ladies smiled at them all.

"Right," said one of them. "Which three want to go first?"

"Me!" they all replied at once.

After make-up, Trudy escorted them all to the TV studio itself. By now it was full of people. There were camera operators standing and sitting next to cameras everywhere, and loads of people with clipboards!

"OK," said Trudy. "This is your cheque, here. . ."

She handed the Glitter Girls an enormous cheque with the amount of four thousand and eight pounds written in big bold lettering.

". . .and this is your one. . ." said Trudy,

handing another cheque to the Scottish girls.

"Now," Trudy explained. "You just sit back and enjoy the programme and I'll come over to cue you for your presentation with Ant and Dec when the time comes." Trudy smiled at them all. "OK?"

"OK!" all of them said at once!

"Remember," Trudy carried on. "ChariTV is a live programme so we need you and all the rest of the audience to scream and cheer as loudly as you can!"

"Go Glitter!" the Glitter Girls screamed in agreement.

"Go Glitter!" their new friends cheered back.

And they all collapsed into giggles.

★ ♥ ★ ♥ ★ ♥ ★

Every one of the Glitter Girls had butterflies in her stomach when Trudy appeared on the floor in front of the cameras accompanied by Ant and Dec. They were ready to begin!

"Good evening, everyone!" said Trudy to the audience.

"Evening!" everyone shouted back and then fell silent.

"Counting down to the start of the programme. . ." Trudy looked at her stopwatch. "Five, four, three, two, one . . . ON AIR!"

ChariTV had begun!

There was loud music, flashing lights, and a huge round of applause as Ant and Dec greeted everyone and explained all about ChariTV and how people could call in to pledge money. On one side of the studio, there were rows and rows of people, all sitting with earphones on, waiting to take people's pledges.

"Isn't this great?" Meg whispered to Charly and Hannah, who were sitting on either side of her.

They both simply squeezed her hands in excitement!

Now the programme had begun in earnest, and there were short films showing all the wonderful things that had been done last year with the money raised, as well as other films explaining all the projects and people that ChariTV hoped to help at home and abroad with the money they hoped this year's programme would raise.

"And now," said Ant, "we welcome Atomic Kitten!"

The audience erupted into cheers as Atomic Kitten began to sing their latest single, live! When they had finished, they did a brief interview with Dec and then they walked off the set, right past the Glitter Girls. One of them – Jenny – winked at them!

"Get her autograph!" Zoe whispered to Flo.

Without hesitation, Flo ran after Jenny and presented her with her special pen and held out her T-shirt. "Could you sign this?" Flo asked.

"Sure!" said Jenny.

And before the Glitter Girls knew it, all of them had T-shirts autographed by all the band!

After that there was a constant stream of people being whisked on and off stage.

The Glitter Girls soon realized that they were sitting in a perfect spot to ask for autographs. All of the stars had to walk past the Glitter Girls on their way out of the studio, so they were able to ask all of them to sign their T-shirts! It was great!

Hannah, Flo, Meg, Zoe and Charly were so engrossed in watching the programme, that they'd forgotten that they were actually taking part. Suddenly Trudy appeared with her clipboard and smiled at them.

"Your turn now!" she smiled.

"Wow!" said Charly, standing up first.

"I'm really nervous," said Hannah excitedly.

"Good luck!" Flo whispered both to the other Glitter Girls and their new friends, all of whom were coming up with them to meet Ant and Dec.

They followed Trudy on to the studio floor.

"And now," said Ant. "It's time to meet some more of you wonderful people who have raised so much cash for us over the last few weeks."

"First, we have five young ladies from Scotland who have been busy swimming around the clock," said Dec.

There was enormous applause as the Scottish girls spoke with Ant and Dec and explained all about their swimming relay. They even showed some film footage of the girls' epic swim.

Then Dec turned to the Glitter Girls and said, "And these are the Glitter Girls and they've come to hand us a cheque on behalf of Wells Road School. They organized a fantastic Auction of Promises and raised loads of money and lots of laughs – as this film will show you. . ."

The Glitter Girls watched as the clips of Mr Eng's video appeared on a huge screen.

After more applause from the audience, Ant spoke briefly with all of the girls as they explained how much fun the Auction was.

"Now," said Dec. "A little bird has told us that one of you girls is after our job!"

"Yes, we were talking to Natalie – Sonia from *EastEnders* – earlier. . ." explained Ant.

The Glitter Girls gasped as they realized he was talking about Charly wanting to be a television presenter!

"So which of you is it then, girls?" Dec asked.

Hannah, Flo, Meg and Zoe looked on happily as Charly stepped forward bravely and said, "Me!"

"So, you're Charly, are you?" Ant asked.

Charly nodded.

"Well – you're about to get your first job! Can you read that screen over there for us?"

Charly could hardly believe what was happening. She took a deep breath and faced the camera.

"And now, ladies and gentlemen, we are going over to our studio in Wales to find out from Sîan what fund-raising activities have been happening there today!"

Charly beamed at the other Glitter Girls. She had just had her first real experience as a television presenter, and she loved it!

★ ♥ ★ ♥ ★ ♥ ★

On the train home, much later that night, the Glitter Girls felt a mixture of pleasure and total exhaustion. It had been the most fantastic day! Looking down at their T-shirts, the Glitter Girls were in too much of a daze to take in exactly how many famous people had signed them.

"Well – was it as good as you thought it would be?" Mrs Wadhurst asked.

"Better!" the Glitter Girls all replied at once.

"I was so proud of you all!" said Miss Stanley, smiling at them. "And as for you Charly! A presenter on live television!"

Charly beamed back. "It was great!" she exclaimed.

"It was great!" said Zoe.

"Yes! Ant and Dec were so nice!" agreed Hannah.

"And so was Sonia, I mean – Natalie!" said Charly, laughing.

"Everything was so cool!" said Meg, sighing.

"But how on earth are we going to beat ChariTV for excitement?" asked Flo.

Meg sat back in her seat and smiled. "Oh, I'm sure we'll manage to think of something," she said.

"Go Glitter!" they all cried.

Don't miss:

Fashion Show Fun

It was Saturday afternoon and the Glitter Girls were at Hannah's house. They'd spent a brilliant morning shopping at one of their favourite places, Girl's Dream, and now they were back, the girls were busy discussing all the gorgeous things they'd seen.

"Aren't those matching jeans and jackets just fantastic?" Zoe asked the others.

"Oh, they're so cool!" agreed Hannah. "I love that pink silvery denim!"

"I've never seen material like that, ever!" Meg sighed, wistfully.

"And those T-shirts were fab," said Flo.

"I want all of them!" Charly said dreamily, as she flicked through the pages of a magazine.

"Hey, look," exclaimed Flo, peering over Charly's shoulder. "There's that crop top we saw!"

"Oh yes," said Charly. "Isn't it beautiful? You'd look great in that Flo!"

"Thanks, Charly," said Flo. "I'll just have to save up my pocket money – I want everything in Girl's Dream!"

"Me too!" agreed Meg.

"I don't believe it!" Charly exclaimed suddenly.

"What?" asked Hannah.

"This!" said Charly excitedly, pointing at an article in the magazine.

As the Glitter Girls were leaving Girl's Dream they'd each been given a copy of a special magazine. It was called *Girl's Dream*, just like the shop, and it was packed full of articles about fashion, make-up, music and everything that was sold in the Glitter Girls' favourite shop.

"What is it?" asked Hannah.

Charly had a very big grin across her face. "They're having a fashion competition!" she said.

★ ♥ ★ ♥ ★ ♥ ★

"Let's see!" the others all cried at once, as they quickly gathered round the magazine that was now spread out on the floor in front of Charly.

Charly read the details of the competition to the others.

"It says that they're holding a fashion show in London!" she said, scanning down to read some more. "And the clothes are going to be all new outfits that haven't been seen before. . ."

"Wow!" said Zoe, imagining how big her wardrobe would have to be if she was lucky enough to own all the clothes in Girl's Dream.

". . .and one of the outfits is going to be designed. . ." Meg continued, ". . .by THE WINNER OF THE COMPETITION!"

"What a cool prize!" said Flo.

"Fantastic!" agreed Hannah.

"What do we have to do?" asked Zoe.

Charly quickly read through the rules and then said, "We've got to design an outfit and then send the design in with a photograph of the designer.

"And the winning outfit will be made up and sold in the shops!" Charly read on. "And as well as the overall winner, thirty runners up will have the chance to model at the fashion show in London!"

"Excellent!" said Flo.

"What's the closing date for entries?" asked Zoe.

Charly looked down at the magazine again. "The 24th – that's two weeks from today!"

"We've got to go for it!" said Flo.

"Flo's right!" agreed Hannah. "We've got to enter!"

"Go Glitter!" the others agreed.

★　❤　★　❤　★　❤　★

"So what are we going to design then?" Zoe asked.

"Bootleg trousers!"

"A mini-skirt!"

"Dungarees!" shouted Flo, Hannah and Charly all at once.

"We've got to agree on one thing if we're going to enter this together," laughed Meg. "So what shall we design?"

"How about a skirt with a matching top and jacket," suggested Flo.

"But why do we all have to do the one outfit?" asked Zoe. "I mean – can't we all send in our own?"

"I suppose we could. . ." replied Meg. "But I thought we were going to enter together – make it a team effort?"

"What does it say in the rules?" asked Charly.

"Yes," said Hannah, flicking her long red hair back behind her ears. "Is there anything to say that we can't enter together? That way we could design a complete wardrobe of clothes that all co-ordinate with each other."

"Cool!" said Flo, popping her thumb in her mouth as she started thinking some more about the outfit she wanted to design.

Meg started reading the rules of the competition.

". . .It doesn't say anything about a group entering," she said.

"What do you think we should do?" Zoe wondered, fiddling with her butterfly hairclip.

"Well," said Meg, smiling at her friend. "It doesn't say that we can't, does it? I think we should put in a group entry – a complete wardrobe of clothes designed with Glitter Girl style!"

"Brilliant!" Zoe grinned.

"Yes," agreed Charly. "That's a great idea!"

"Well," said Flo, "what are we waiting for? Let's get going!"

"What do we need to do?" asked Charly.

Meg read out the rules. "It says 'Entrants must design a complete outfit with accessories, including shoes'."

"Does that mean bags as well?" Zoe wondered.

"I think so," said Meg.

"Great!" said Flo. "So – how do we present our designs?"

Meg looked at the magazine again. "Umm – we need to draw our designs on a sheet of A4 paper, and put our names and addresses on the back. Oh – and we've got to send in a colour photograph of each of us as well!"

"What do they want those for?" Hannah wondered.

"To see if they think we'd make good models I suppose," said Charly.

"Well, we'd better get started then," said Meg.

"I've got lots of A4 sketch paper at home," said Flo. "I could go home and get it. And I can bring along some felt pens and pencils."

And that's just what she did!

★ ❤ ★ ❤ ★ ❤ ★

Ten minutes later there was a RAT-tat-tat! at the bedroom door.

"Who is it?" Hannah whispered from behind her bedroom door.

"GG!" came the reply. Hannah opened her bedroom door and Flo hurried in, carrying two huge carrier bags.

"I've brought a load of rough paper and my best block of paper," said Flo, pulling out a large pad of thick cartridge paper from one of the bags.

"Are you sure you don't mind us using it?" Charly asked.

"Course not – I mean you're only going to use one sheet each, aren't you?" said Flo. "We'll do our first sketches on our rough paper and then, when we're happy with everything we can do our finished drawings."

"Right," said Meg, opening her notebook. "Who's going to design what?

"Bags I do the mini-skirt," said Hannah.

"Can I do dungarees?" asked Charly.

"Oh, I just can't decide. . ." said Flo, plaintively. ". . .OK, I think it's got to be the bootleg trousers and jacket."

Meg wrote it all down.

"And what will you do, Zoe?" she asked.

"I'm going to design a dress," Zoe said, already thinking of the great accessories that she could put with it.

"OK . . . I think I'd like to try a coat," said Meg.

"Sorted then!" said Flo. "Shall we get started?"

"Go Glitter!"